THE MURDER OF RITA REILEY, PLUS ONE

by Ed Folino

The Murder of Rita Reiley, Plus One
by Ed Folino
Copyright ©2018 Ed Folino

ISBN : 9781633600775
For Worldwide Distribution
Printed in the U.S.A.

List of characters included in this story

Pete Patrone   Rookie detective sergeant & narrator
John Folino   Veteran detective sergeant
Gino & Rosa Folino   John Folino's parents
Capt. Jack Elam   Allentown police captain
Rita Mancuso   Allentown secretary
Rita Reiley   The murder victim
Jean Reiley Forbes   Rita's step-sister
Frank Forbes   Jean Reiley's husband
Elsie   Rita & Jean's mother
Jack Frey   The married businessman
Mona Frey   The wife of John Frey
Cheryl Hauser   Secretary in Jack Frey's office
Gino Regerio   Rita's boss and owner of Joe's bar
Stephen Ross   Rita's former lover
Jerry Hicks   Slime ball ex-con
Louis Scott   Carrick High School Principal
Roger Matthews   High school senior
Bill Evans   Rita's across the street neighbor
Omar Pack   Rita's next door neighbor
Dr. Steve Peterson   Coroner and head of forensics team
Linda Peterson   Dr. Peterson's assistant [no relation]
Johnny Stanko   Bar patron at Joe's Bar
Eddie Edosia   Bar patron at Joe's Bar
Judge Amy Austin   Judge who issued warrant
Harry Goldstein   Attorney for Jean Reiley
Ruth Rubridge   Allegheny County District Attorney

THE MURDER OF
RITA REILEY, PLUS ONE

Rita Reiley was a substitute school teacher working for The Pittsburgh Board of Education. Rita was a petite five-feet-three, with fiery red hair that cascaded over her shoulders. I guess she could have been a beauty queen if she put her mind to it; she was that pretty. She chose the field of education because she really wanted to be a teacher. She was a sought after substitute teacher by not the faculty at Brashear High School, but by the students, especially the boys. The girls liked her because she gave them fashion and etiquette tips that they used in their daily lives. The boys liked her because she was a pretty woman that they could fantasize about – you know, someone to get their testosterone level sailing. There was one student, though, that really scared Rita, Roger Mathews. Roger was a huge boy who was on his second attempt at graduating. He failed terribly at summer school and was told that he had to repeat twelfth grade all over again. Roger was about six-foot-three and weighed a good three hundred pounds. He was a scrapper that nobody messed with. He also had a thing for Rita and he wasn't afraid to tell her. She turned him into the disciplinary board a few times, but nothing was ever done about him. I think they were all afraid of Roger, including the school staff.

Because of an impasse in the state budget due to the election of a new governor, there were little monies for any advanced or even simple education studies. Rita chose to supplement her teaching work by moonlighting nights at Joe's tavern, a local hangout. Rita's boss at Joe's was the owner, Gino Rigerio. Gino was a slob who had no respect for women at all. He was constantly and intentionally bumping into Rita and belittling her in front of the customers, especially the women customers, who frequented Joe's. Joe's was not a nice place to hang out at and its clientele reflected on their shoddy reputation. The only reason Gino hired Rita was because she drew in the male clientele who spent a lot of money. The men who frequented Joe's sure weren't coming there to see Gino. He had a few friends, but they were as dippy as him. The only reason Rita worked at Joe's was because it was close to home and the extra pay helped subsidize what she was making with the City of Pittsburgh. A few times Rita got up the nerve to talk back to Gino. He accepted that backtalk because he feared that Rita would quit and he would lose the business she generated. He also knew that his business wouldn't survive with his crappy personality alone.

Rita had a step-sister, Jean, whom she loved dearly. Jean was the result of Rita's mother's second marriage. Jean was married to a pig of a man, Frank. We'll get more into him later. Rita and Jean's mother, Elsie, was a lovely woman who everyone adored. Her first husband, Roy, was a fine man who died from a massive heart attack at forty three. Elsie's second husband, Oscar, was an alcoholic who frequently beat Elsie. Fortunately he died an early death from an enlarged liver due to alcoholism, no doubt. Rita and Jean loved their mother dearly and took great care of her during her early retirement years. Elsie was an elementary school teacher; I think that's why Rita chose the field of education as her vocation in her life. It's a shame Elsie didn't live long enough to enjoy the benefits of a young widow enjoying life; she died at sixty-one from a brain aneurism.

After Elsie's death Jean and Rita became closer, often staying up half the night talking to each other on the phone. They also did the Facebook thing and communicated by e-mail.

My name is Pete Patrone, and I'm a sergeant for the Pittsburgh Police Department, also known as PPD. I studied criminal law at the University of Pittsburgh and received my degree in criminal law, with a minor in communications. I'm originally from Chicago, but I had heard about the excellent program that Pitt University offered in its criminal law school. After graduation I was assigned to the homicide division of the PPD's/Allentown Squad. I was partnered with a veteran of the force, Sergeant John Folino. John had been with the force for almost 25 years. He knew the city well and also knew all its charms and let me put it this way, non-charms. The major charm of Pittsburgh was its bridges that connected the communities to the downtown area of Pittsburgh and its friendly people. The major un-charm of Pittsburgh was the ugliness of crime, of which I chose to pursue as my vocation in life. I suppose Pittsburgh had a similar crime reputation as Chicago, but on a smaller scale. One thing I can truthfully say about Pittsburgh is the friendliness of its people—you can always tell if a person was from Pittsburgh—they're friendly and they'll say hello to you, even if they don't know you. I can't say that for Chicago—if anything, Chicagoans are very standoffish. My partner, John, would frequently drive us to Grandview Avenue, the home of observation decks looking down on this beautiful city. When I invited friends or relatives in from Chicago the observation decks were the first place I would take them. It was a great way to introduce people to the outward beauty of this great city.

A SHORT DETAILED HISTORY
OF JOHN AND ME

John Folino was a veteran of the PPD with almost twenty-five years of service. From talking to a few of John's previous partners I found out that he had a terrible temper, some said volatile at times. I imagine that with the length of service with the department he should have been a Lieutenant by now but I feel it was his temper that held his promotion back. I understand that he attended numerous anger management seminars over the years but with no endearing results. I'm pretty sure that John never pushed the issue of his promotion because, frankly, he was glad to be employed at all with the department. John had an excellent arrest record——I think that this is one of the factors of why he was maintained over the years. John had a couple of boys who he loved dearly. His wife divorced him after the boys had grown and entered college. The department is all he had. I found him to be very diligent in his job and he worried about his partners. [Thank God] He lived in the Mt. Washington section of Pittsburgh, in a small rented home that was not near the observation decks, with their pricy homes and beautiful city views. He was four blocks from the decks——he called his neighborhood the cheap section of Mt. Washington. I liked John. We investigated a few murders together but never to the conviction. We'd testify at numerous murder trials but that was as far as it went. Beings that I was somewhat of a rookie, our Captain, Michael Reese, ordered us to work this case from the initial investigation until the ultimate conviction. He said it would be a good experience for both of us, a seasoned pro and a rookie, hoping to get his feet wet.

I rent a second floor duplex in the outskirts of Pittsburgh called Dormont. It's a nice community with around nine thousand residents according to a 2010 census. It has its share of restaurants, bars, coffee shops, and retail stores. It also has a gigunda outdoor swimming pool which I frequent a few times a week in the summer months. Pittsburgh has a great transit system nicknamed "The T." It runs through Dormont from a few communities south until it arrives in downtown Pittsburgh. Dormont has a small police department of thirteen officers, and an excellent volunteer fire department. From all the negative publicity the last few years about their city council, I'm glad I work for the City of Pittsburgh and not any surrounding communities. I'm happy here and I'm fortunate I'm only fifteen minutes from my station in Allentown. My Father was instrumental in getting me the duplex I currently live in. He is a real estate agent in Chicago and he used his connections from his global company to find me a reasonable priced place. I'm sure he didn't know about the two strippers, Stella and Bella, who occupy the first floor of my duplex. They sort of keep to themselves, and I mean themselves, if you know what I mean.

MURDER

Well, I guess we should get to the matter at hand, a homicide. Unfortunately, John and I were assigned to investigate the murder of Rita Reiley. I say unfortunately because Rita was such a lovely woman that John and I discovered during our investigation. But things are never as they seem. You'll see as the story progresses. John and I treated all of our murder investigations with the same intensity but when the victim was such a well-liked person, it seemed to tug at our hearts more than a victim that had many flaws. Who would have wanted to kill such a lovely lady?

Let's start from the beginning—John and I received a call from Jim Hazlett, a supervisor for the City of Pittsburgh's 911 department. Jim said, "One of my operators received a call from a hysterical woman concerning her sister. She said that she and her sister communicated every night but she was unable to get in touch with her tonight." Jim added, "We would normally tell people who had friends or relatives to wait at least twenty-four hours until reporting them missing, but when the circumstances of Rita's disappearance was explained to me, I felt concerned. All she wanted was for a couple of officers to drive to Rita's residence and see if she was there, and was all right." I told our operator that I was going to send a few policeman to check on Rita. Jean also pointed out to the operator that she was confined to a wheelchair and was unable to check on Rita herself because she didn't drive.

I told Mr. Hazlett I'd see what I could do. We contacted our captain and received the okay to take a drive to Rita's residence and check things out. Jim said, "When Jean called she pointed out that she tried to contact her husband, Frank, at the various watering holes he frequented because he conveniently forgot his cell phone at home. Jean told me that she could not contact her sister in any way, by phone, e-mail, or Nextel. Jean and Rita had a Nextel system where they could communicate instantly and there was no response using that either. Jean told me that Rita told her that she was feeling depressed lately and was going to take off her shift at Joe's Tavern and was going to spend the night at home. John and I gassed up a four wheel drive Jeep and began our nasty trip. I say nasty because there were about twelve inches of snow on the ground and it was still coming down pretty good. Rita's home was in the Mt. Washington section of the city which was surrounded by many steep hills. The City of Pittsburgh doesn't have too well of a reputation for snow removal, but in their defense, I think they're waiting for the snow to slow down before they begin their salting procedures. Also, Rita's house is considered located on a secondary road which aren't salted until all the main roads are. Right after we left the station we received a call from our captain, Jack Johnson, who said, "It looks like you guys may be investigating a murder. The 911 department received another call regarding Rita Reiley. The caller, a Bill Evans, called to report a possible murder at Ms. Reiley's address. He stated that he saw a bloodied body on the floor through an open front door of Ms. Reiley's house. I told him that you and John were on your way, and to not touch anything at the scene."

THE INVESTIGATION

It was a really nasty night for traveling but we had to get to Rita's house to investigate this murder, if in fact there had been a murder. The main roads were icy and the side roads were snow covered with ice beneath them— the worst kind of winter driving scenario. Good old City of Pittsburgh maintenance, shirking their responsibilities again. It took us almost an hour to arrive at Rita's house. There was a car running in the front of Rita's with two men inside. We soon discovered that the men in the car were Bill Evans, who reported the crime, and Omar Pack, a retired

Pittsburgh police officer, who was a neighbor of Rita's. He lived next door. As soon as we arrived on the scene, the two men emerged from the car. We decided to question them separately in case there was any collusion involved in this alleged crime. John said that he would interview Bill Evans, while I would question Omar Pack.

JOHN'S INTERVIEW
WITH BILL EVANS

John formally introduced himself to Bill Evans. He told Bill that Pete and he were investigating a possible murder of Rita Reiley based on his 911 phone call. John asked Bill at what time he saw Rita's door open.

Bill said "It was 10:45 when he noticed that Rita's front door was wide open."

I asked Bill how he remembered that it was 10:45.

He said, "I remember looking at my watch and it read 10:45. I checked the time because I like to get the dog home by 11PM so I can watch the nightly news."

John said, "According to the 911 report you looked in Rita's house and saw her lying on the floor and that her body appeared to be bloodied. Tell me Bill, why did you look in Rita's home?"

Bill said "I didn't know Rita that well but I knew that she was a schoolteacher and worked at Joe's Bar down the road. I didn't loaf at Joe's but I stopped there a few times to pick up a six pack or some hot sausage sandwiches. The temp outside was around fifteen degrees—why would anyone have their front door open in that kind of weather? Bill added, and from what I've learned from other neighbors, Rita pretty much kept to herself——I never saw her with any boyfriends."

John said, "I didn't ask you about Rita's love life. Why did you volunteer that info, Bill?"

Bill replied, "I've seen enough cop shows on TV and when there is a single woman involved, the cops always ask a witness if the woman had any boyfriends. Oh, by the way, they have some dynamite hot sausages at Joe's."

I told Bill that I wasn't really interested in hot sausage at the moment but if I had time Pete and I may stop after we were done here. I asked Bill how he ended up in Omar Pack's car.

Bill replied, "I knew that Omar was a retired police officer and I knocked on his door hoping he could give me some advice on what to do after discovering Rita's body. I almost gave up on trying to contact Omar because it took him so long for him to answer the door. After all it was only 10:45 in the evening and I figured it was too early for him to be in bed. He did apologize for taking so long to get to the door and added it took him so long because he had a virus and had taken a sleep aid to try and get some much needed shot eye. It was Omar who offered to get his car and wait for you guys to come."

I said, "Why didn't he ask you to wait in his house for us?"

Bill said, "I did mention it, but he said his house was a mess and that he would pull his car to the front of Rita's house. He also pointed out that he had a big old Cadillac and that the heater blasted out some very wicked hot air."

John asked Bill if Omar said anything else to him while they were waiting in the car.

"He told me not to touch anything at the crime

scene", Bill said.

John told Bill that was all he had for him now and thanked him for calling 911 and getting involved. He also told him that he may be calling on him for additional questions when he may need to visit us at our Allentown precinct.

MY INTERVIEW WITH OMAR PACK

Omar was a large man—I would say around three to three hundred and fifty pounds. Hey, when they're that big what's another twenty or thirty pounds? Omar told us about his retired status with the Pittsburgh Police Department when we initially pulled in front of Rita' house. I didn't want to mention his excessive weight to him but I figured like other retirees, he just let himself go. I asked him about his work history with the PPD.

Omar said, "I was in the homicide division. I started there thirty years ago and retired from that department two years ago. That is how I was able to advise Bill on what to do in regards to Rita's murder, if in fact she was murdered. I mean, with all of that blood splattered all over her floor, it would have to be a murder. There was always the possibility of a suicide but that would really be a stretch. Besides that, I knew Rita and I know that she wouldn't be the type of person to commit suicide."

I thanked Omar for his time and help with our investigation. I told him I would most likely be getting back to him. Now John and I had to wait for the Coroner and the forensics team. I don't know what crew was coming but whoever it is will not be happy trudging out here at this time of night. John and I thought we'd check out the scene and take some more notes.

THE CRIME [MURDER] SCENE

We entered through the open door of Rita's house. Boy, there was a lot of blood! I looked at John and saw that he appeared a little queasy. I asked him if he was okay and he said, "I've seen plenty of bloody murder scenes and you would think I'd be used to them by now but you never do. I can tell you one thing, this is definitely a murder scene and not a suicide. From my initial observation, no one can stab themselves eight to ten times in a suicide attempt."

There was a blood trail coming from what we discovered was the kitchen. The trail continued on through the dining room, where a few chairs had been obviously knocked over and then on to the front hallway of Rita's house. With our gloves on, John and I tipped the body over a little because we both thought that Rita was lying on something and we were right. There was a large knife protruding from Rita's side. I'm not a knife expert, but the handle looked like the ones that people had in their kitchens. Our suspicions were confirmed when we observed a large kitchen knife missing from an eight piece set that was hung on the kitchen wall. John had a theory of which I agreed.

He said, "From the amount of blood in the kitchen, it looked like Rita was stabbed there and made her way to the front hallway of her house and collapsed, hoping to escape from her assailant. I'm not a medical expert but from the amount of blood lost, it looked like the murderer hit a main artery. And it appears the murderer entered through the jimmied back door. Rita must have been watching TV in the living room and must have heard a noise in the kitchen. When Rita entered the kitchen the assailant must have stabbed her. My partner, Pete Patrone found a fireplace poker on the floor of the kitchen. I assumed that when Rita heard the noise in the kitchen, she grabbed the poker for protection before entering the kitchen."

THE CORONER ARRIVES WITH HIS TEAM

The coroner, Dr. Steve Peterson and his assistant Linda Peterson, no relation to Steve, arrived about an hour later. John questioned Dr. Peterson on why there were only two members of the forensics team.

The Doc said, "Twenty years ago, on a case like this, we would have a five or six member team but with all the budget cuts in the city lately, we get two—the coroner and my assistant, Linda.

John and I gave Dr. Peterson a written copy of some of our thoughts and ideas on the case. We told him that we were going to drive down the road to interview Gino Rigerio, the owner of Joe's bar and Rita's boss. In those notes we said that the back door was jimmied, indicating the killer probably didn't know Rita. We also observed that there were no footprints in the front or rear of the house because of all the snow that dropped the last six or seven hours. We told the doctor we would see him at the station the next day and to contact us when he had any info on the case. I wonder how long those two have been working together, because they sure did act chummy. We left the good doctor and his assistant at the crime scene to do their thing.

OUR INTERVIEW WITH
GINO RIGERIO
[OWNER OF JOE'S BAR]

We drove up the road to Joe's Bar. It was located on Grandview Avenue where some of the observation decks were located, where people gazed at this beautiful city. This area was called Mt. Washington, or The Mount, which is what a lot of the locales referred to it. Joe's was located across the street from the expensive restaurants which also provided a great view of the city. In our conversation with Gino, he told us that he was approached by numerous realtors to purchase his bar but he was holding out for more money. I'm sure when someone bought this dump they'd tear it down and build a nice respectable establishment. Bill Evans was correct when he said that it was just down the road from Rita's house. It actually was close enough to Rita's that she could probably walk there from her house but not in this kind of crappy weather. It was about 1:30 AM when we entered Joe's and there were only two men sitting at an old oak bar. The man behind the bar didn't look like Gino Rigerio—he looked more like Morty Freeman. He had blonde kinky hair and a snozzola that would stop a tractor trailer. I mean, that sucker was huge. John and I walked up to him and asked if Gino Rigerio was working tonight.

He said, "I'm Gino Rigerio. Who are you?"

By then John and I had taken out our police badges.

Gino said, "I **thought** you were cops, because you look like cops."

I could tell from the way this guy was talking that

he was a dipshit. I said "Oh yea, what's a cop look like?"

He said, "You guys always look tired—you are both wearing a suit coming into a dump like this, and, I swear to God, you all buy your topcoats at the same Policemen's Topcoat Store."

I said, "Well wise guy, you don't look like a Gino, you look more like a Morty or a Saul. Were you adopted?" I could tell he was pissed.

John was standing right behind me and said softly, but loud enough for Gino to hear, "Even though the guy's a jerk, take it easy on him, Pete."

Gino looked at John and I and said, "Getting back to the Gino, Morty crack, my late mother was one hundred percent Jewish and my Dad one hundred percent Sicilian Italian. As you can see, I've taken my looks from my mother's side of the family."

Behind me John said, "Boy, I'll say!"

Gino got his Jewish/Dago up and said, "You know, I can throw you two out of my bar, cops or no cops."

I said, "I don't think you can but let's get down to the reason of why we are here and it isn't for your hot sausage. It appears that one of your employees was murdered tonight."

Gino said, "That's a no brainer, Buster—I only have one employee, Rita Reiley."

I said, "That's the one."

"Murdered?"

Yep, "That's what I said, murdered."

The two guys that were sitting at the bar suddenly got off their stools and started to head towards the door. I looked at John and he immediately told both of them to sit back down because we would have a few questions for them.

Gino said, "You guys are really pissing me off— now you're harassing my customers."

I said, "At this early stage of the crime, everyone is a suspect, even you, Gino."

Gino says, "Are you kidding me? I've been here working all night and those two fellas are my witnesses."

"Pretty convenient," I said. "You have your own in house alibis. I have some preliminary questions for you and my partner John will question your two costumers, separately, if that's okay with you. In the meantime, I just realized that my partner and I were getting pretty hungry. Can we still get a couple of hot sausage sandwiches? One of your customers, Bill Evans, said you had the best hot sausage on the Mount. (Although I didn't see any other places around that would be competition for him)

"Bill Evans—what's he got to do with this," Gino said?

I said, "Just get our sandwiches and then I'll have a few questions for you." I was going to ask him if he put the sausage on an Italian roll or a bagel, but I didn't want to aggravate him more than he already was. I went over where John was sitting with the two bar patrons and told him I ordered him a hot sausage. He thanked me and said, "Is it on a bun or a bagel?" Hey great minds think alike. John said that after he got his sausage and ate it, he would question the two bar patrons.

(I know that some of you readers are wondering why I've been giving orders and instructions to John when I am the rookie, and John has twenty-five years with the force. Well, it was agreed at the beginning of this investigation that I would be the lead detective on the case. Captain Johnson wanted to see how I would handle a murder case as the lead detective on the case, if in fact, it was a murder case. Well it turns out it is. A few minutes later Gino came out of a back room with two huge hot sausage sandwiches on Italian rolls with melted cheese overflowing from the plate. I hope they're good, because they sure do look good. I said to Gino, "I see you're the chief cook and bottle washer here!"

Gino said, "Yep, I had to cook the sausages because Rita stiffed me. I had to bartend, wait tables, and cook as well."

I said, "Geno, you pig, give the woman a break, she's dead! I'm sure she'd rather be alive and working in this dump than laying in back of a meat wagon on the way to the morgue."

Geno apologized and said that I was right. He also said that he was exhausted from a long day and night at the Club Sausage. (My wording) I finished my sandwich with a Diet Coke. Bill Evans was right—it really was a good hot sausage sandwich. I told Gino that I was going to check with my partner, John, and that I would be back to take some additional info from him.

I went to the corner of the bar where John was sitting with the two nervous patrons. They didn't know that they could have left—I know John or I weren't going to tell them. I asked John how he was doing and he told me he just finished his delicious hot sausage and he was going to question the two men separately, immediately. I asked him their names so I could add them to my little notebook. No, modern technology had not reached the Allentown police department. Sure we had our share of computers at the station but when we were on the road, we used the dependable pencil and paper. All the info we wrote down was transferred to the main computer when we arrived back at the station. I know it would be a lot more efficient if we had mobile devices but that's the way they wanted to do it and who was I to buck the authorities. Getting back to the two patrons, their names were, Johnny Stanko and Eddie Edosia. I told John to do his thing while I went back to question Gino again.

JOHN FOLINO'S INTERVIEW OF THE TWO BAR PATRONS — FIRST UP, JOHNNY STANKO

John asked Johnny Stanko if he would join him at a corner table of the bar and he agreed. John said, "Mr. Stanko, this will only take a few minutes or more to ask you a few questions. First of all, can I call you Johnny? And after that can I ask you where you work?

"No problem calling me Johnny. Eddie and I are both boilermakers but we are laid off for the winter. The boilermaker local has an excellent savings plan and we spend most of our savings at Joe's"

I said, "I don't think you can spend all your money from this great savings plan on beer and hot sausage, can you?"

Johnny said, "There is more to do than drink beer and eat hot sausages. I don't know if I should be telling you this, but Gino, the owner, also takes our bets on the Pa. lottery, and sports games——it depends on what season it is——he'll book any sport. And, I don't pick too many winners."

I asked Johnny how long he was at the bar this

evening.

He said, "I arrived here at 7PM to watch the Pittsburgh Pens game with Eddie. He didn't get here until 8PM when the game started."

I asked him if there were any other patrons in the bar when he and Eddie were there.

He said, "It's a Sunday night and it's normally pretty quiet after the dinner hour, 5 o'clock, so there wasn't anyone else here when I arrived, just Gino. I was wondering where Rita was, because she usually closes up on Sunday nights. Hey, are you guys here because something happened to Rita?"

I said, "I'm sorry Johnny but I can't discuss anything about the case with you. The only thing I **can** say is that Rita was found murdered tonight. Getting back to how long you were here tonight—how long was it?"

Johnny said, "Seven PM like I told you, until one thirty when you and your partner came in. And I've seen enough detective shows to know that you're going to ask me if I ever left the bar between the times of seven and when you arrived, and the answer is no."

I said, "Wow, six and a half hours and you're still coherent."

Johnny said, "We nursed the beers because we knew we were going to be here all night. The game was over at eleven-thirty and then we shot some pool for an about an hour and then came back to the bar. We had just sat down when you and your partner arrived."

I said, "Okay pal, you can leave now but I may have some additional questions for you in the next couple of days. Let me have your phone number and your e-mail address and will you please send your buddy, Eddie, over because I have to question him now. One thing stuck in my mind about my questioning of Johnny, "He never acted surprised or showed any remorse or sadness when I told him that Rita had been murdered. In fact, he was totally emotionless.

Strange, very strange.

JOHN FOLINO'S QUESTIONING OF EDDIE EDOSIA

Eddie came over and introduced himself with, "Hi, I'm Edward D. Edosia."

I said "Can I call you Eddie?"

He said, "Why not buster? Everyone else does."

I thought to myself, "Just what I need—a jerk with an attitude." Now that I got a good look at Eddie, I noticed he was wearing two earrings on each ear, and, are you ready for this? He was wearing make-up! Maybe this guy wasn't playing for our team.

I asked Eddie if he was at the bar all evening, or to be more specific, what hours was he there this evening?

He said, "I was here at 7PM until you and your partner entered."

I asked Eddie if he left the bar at all during the evening. All of his answers were pretty much the same as Johnny's except when he told me that Johnny arrived at 8PM, not 7PM. I didn't point this out to him but now I'm wondering what Johnny was doing for that hour and why did he lie to me? I'm thinking to myself again, "Geeze, Eddie doesn't talk girlish or gay!" A statement like that would most likely get me suspended or thrown off the force.

I thought I'd go in the other direction with Eddie. I asked him how well he knew Rita and did he sit down to urinate? There I go again—thank God I didn't ask him the urinating question—I only thought it!

Eddie said, "She didn't like Johnny at all."

I said, "I didn't ask you about Johnny, pal."

"Okay," Eddie shot back. "I asked her a few times if she would go out with me and she threatened to call my wife and tell her that I was harassing her, plus a few other things."

Damn, you never know—I would have thought that Eddie was playing for the other side, but as it turns out, he may be playing for our side or even more bizarre—he's playing for both sides. I got this guy's sexual orientation wrong—maybe he and Johnny are playing on the same side and they're teammates. I guess I should concentrate more on trying to find Rita's murderer than trying to figure out who's who in the gender game. I asked Eddie if Gino ever asked Rita to go out.

"Sure," he replied. "Every guy in here has tried, and probably a few women too."

Here I go thinking to myself again. "What the hell kind of place is this?"

"I'm just interested if Gino ever had anything to do with Rita", I queried, Eddie.

"Yea, a few times when she first started. After she turned him down a few times, he made life miserable working here. I guess she needed a job pretty bad to put up with his crap. You know, Detective, you never even mentioned that Rita was murdered tonight. I just happened to hear you talking to Gino. Why is that?"

"Well Eddie", I said. "I didn't mention that to

Gino—it was Detective Patrone, and he didn't say that Rita was murdered—he said to Gino that Rita was dead." The more I thought about it, Pete did tell Gino that Rita was murdered. Regardless, it didn't bother Eddie. He just said, "Whatever!" I told Eddie the same thing that I told his pal, Johnny, that we would probably be contacting them again in a couple days for more questioning. I went over to Pete and saw that he was ready to go. I was tired and I'm sure he was as well. It had been a long day and tomorrow is another one. It was almost 2PM and I asked John if he wanted to meet for lunch, say 12PM.

John said, "That will be fine but let me pick the place, Pete. We are going to a place in Pittsburgh commonly referred to as 'The Strip.' I'll tell you more about it when I see you tomorrow. As far as directions go, just put #46 18th street in your GPS—it's only about ten to fifteen minutes from the Allentown station."

AN UNEXPECTED DETOUR

We left Joe's to pick up our cars at the station when I asked John, "Do you think we could see anything from those observation decks with all the snow blowing around?

John said, "I think so, Pete, I don't think they'll be a big crowd there at 2AM.

Of course, John was correct—the observation deck we visited was tourist free. A lot of the buildings leave their lights on at night, plus you could see the outline of the lights on the parkways. It was an awesome sight, not as nice as during the day but still an amazing sight. After driving a couple of blocks from the observation deck, we spotted a guy trying to change a flat tire. We were both exhausted but we couldn't just pass him up without checking out the situation. We pulled up behind the disabled car and got out of our nicely warmed up Jeep. John asked the guy if he needed a hand changing the tire.

The guy says, "I wish you guys would have been here a half hour ago—you could have changed it for me. Ah, I'm just kidding. Actually, I'm almost done—I had to put one of those jelly donut replacement tires on."

I discounted the guy's attempt at humor and asked him what he was doing there this time of night—maybe he was coming home from work. I don't think he was making a social visit with the really crappy weather we were experiencing. I was starting to not like this guy for some reason. I decided to ask him for his license and owner's card. It turned out he was Frank Forbes, Rita's brother-in-law and Jean's husband. What are the odds we run into him at this time of night and this close to Rita's house?

I looked at Frank and said, "Frank Forbes, do you know that we know you?"

Frank says, "How the hell do you know me?"

I said, "You're Frank Forbes and you're Jean Reiley Forbes husband. Now, what the hell are you doing here this time of night? At this point I realized that I smelled alcohol on his breath. In all the confusion John and I failed to give him the test—of course that was before we knew who he was. I asked John to get the breathalyzer kit out of the Jeep. All of our vehicles are equipped with the kits. In the meantime, I asked Frank where he was going at this late hour.

He said, "I made a few stops at some of my favorite joints and decided I'd stop at my sister-in-law's and see how she was doing. I only had a beer or two at each joint. Can I tell you something off the record officer?"

"Sure you can Frank, I won't tell a soul." I'm thinking to myself, "Maybe this guy is loaded to be asking me a stupid question like that."

Frank says, "If you know my wife, you know that she's confined to a wheelchair and isn't able to satisfy my needs, if you know what I mean. So, from time to time I stop at her sister Rita's for a little companionship, if you know what I mean."

Repeating himself—one of the classic signs that he may be intoxicated. I said, "Yea, Frank, unfortunately, I know what you mean. Well I'll tell you one thing, you won't be seeking Rita for anymore companionship—she was found dead tonight. Are you sure you are not coming from her house and not on your way to her house as you said?"

"No, officer," Frank said. I hit a few joints like I said and being the upstanding citizen that I am, I took a nap in my car for about an hour. Besides that, the roads were pretty bad at Joe's tavern."

"Are you trying to tell me that you were at Joe's Tavern tonight?"

"No. I wasn't," Frank went on. "I meant to say, Carmen's. Boy, I'm really confused tonight."

"I think you're more than confused, Frank—I think you're under the influence."

John brought the breathalyzer over and administered the test to Frank. Sure as shit, the numbers indicated that Frank was over the legal limit for alcohol consumption. I said, "Okay, Frank, it looks like you're taking a little trip to tour our Allentown facility. I'll call and reserve a nice cell for you. Maybe we'll cook a few burgers for you too. Are you hungry?"

"Yes I am," Frank said. Boy it's really nice of you

guys to feed me burgers."

I just looked at him and said, "Sure." I told Frank that he was going to go in our Jeep to the station. I was going to have him sit in the back seat but John was back there snoring away. I decided I better cuff Frank. When I told him I was going to put cuffs on him he went ballistic.

He started screaming, "What the hell are these for? I may have had a few extra drinks tonight but I don't think you have to put handcuffs on me—they're for holding murderers. Wait a minute, didn't you say Rita was murdered tonight? Are you trying to blame that murder on me?"

I said, "First of all, I never mentioned murder—I just said that she was dead and we're not trying to blame anything on you. How about we get you to the station and you can get some sleep."

"And don't forget the burgers," Frank mused.

"No we won't. Right now we're going to have your car towed to the police pound."

"Let me get a few things out of it first," Frank said.

"I don't think so, Frank. It will have to be searched for evidence once we have it in our garage."

He freaked out again. "Evidence, evidence for what? Don't give me that crap. You think I killed Rita, don't you? Well. I was there tonight, but she was already dead."

With that little piece of info, I thought it was about time to read this dirt bag his rights. John was awake now and I filled him in on everything that Frank had told me. He agreed that we cuff him and have his car towed. We both had to wait for the tow truck, because we couldn't leave Frank's car there on the street unattended. I couldn't believe the tow truck was there in only twenty minutes, with the really sucky weather we were having—I don't think it stopped snowing since we left the station. After I thought about it for a minute, I realized that the tow trucks are equipped with chains and would have no trouble maneuvering around in this kind of weather.

We arrived at the station about a half hour later with Frank Forbes in tow. Right now, he looks like our prime suspect but that would be too easy. We brought Frank before the Officer on Duty for the night, Rich Mancuso. Rich was a nice guy, but he could be ignorant at times. After hearing Frank's tale of woe, he said, "Throw him in the slammer!" There's that ignorant factor creeping in. We turned Frank over to the turnkey and headed toward our cars. I told John that I would meet him at the station around noon instead of at the restaurant as I previously said. I figured why should two of us get stuck in the snow, although the City of Pittsburgh were salt blitzing all the streets by now and they may be passable.

A DIFFERENT KIND OF LUNCH

As I predicted the streets were in pretty good shape in the morning. I arrived at the station at 11:45 AM and stopped by the Coroner's lab. I guess I should have knocked, because the good doctor and his assistant looked like they had just got done playing Mommy and Daddy. Their clothes were in complete disarray. I think they may have been screwing around or a twister flew through a window and blew their clothes around. Doc Peterson was calm and cool but his assistant, Linda Peterson, [remember—no relation] was as red as a beet. I said, "Did I catch you at a bad time, Doc?"

He said, "Not really, detective, I was just teaching

Ms. Peterson a new technique I've been using for performing autopsies."

Boy, you would think he'd come up with a better excuse than that.

"If you're here about the Reiley murder, the autopsy is not complete yet. After all it was very late when I was called to her house last night and I didn't get a lot of sleep."

I'm thinking to myself, "He didn't get a lot of sleep—he was probably playing house with his assistant. I wonder if his wife, Gina, knows about his extracurricular activities. Hey, I could be wrong—nah, I know I'm right."

I looked at the Doc, and said, "I'm in no hurry for the Reiley results—I'm meeting John Folino in a few minutes and he's taking me to some place called "The Strip."

The Doc said, "Well I'm sure you'll find something good to eat down there. Hey, ask John if he could pick up a sandwich for Linda, I mean Ms. Peterson, and I. Anything he gets will be fine. I'm starving and I know Ms. Peterson is as well."

Yea, they're both starving—probably from the workout they just had. I told the Doc that John and I would get him something to eat and that we would probably be back around 2PM.

I met John at precisely 12PM, boy, I love people that are punctual. We were going to sign out a Jeep when I remembered about our buddy, Frank. I stopped to see if Rich Mancuso was still on duty—he was. I asked him if Frank Forbes was still in a cell.

He said, "No, someone posted his bail about six this morning. You didn't want us to hold him, did you?"

"Well he could be a murder suspect but we don't have enough to hold him yet. Tell me Rich, who paid his bail?"

"It was his wife, Jean Reiley—she seemed like a real nice lady but he seemed like a jerk," Rich said.

I said, "Didn't I understand that she is confined to a wheelchair?"

Rich said, "Yes, she is. It was a real hassle getting her in here. We had to get one of the guys on desk duty to get her out of a cab and into the building. She had another woman with her that was totally useless, but we got it done. I did tell him to stay home because you were probably going to be over and question him today."

John drove to this amazing area outside of downtown Pittsburgh which I assumed was "The Strip." There were restaurants everywhere. Besides the restaurants there were a lot of fruit markets. There were also a ton of places to buy souvenirs. The snow had stopped overnight but it was still in the teens. Even though it was that cold, there were vendors selling everything from Chinese chicken to Italian beef. There were also T-shirt vendors up the ying yang. [That means there were a lot of them] We stopped at one restaurant that served six egg omelets, yea six. I opted for the three egg one—after all, I had to work all day. Every restaurant sign that we saw had a sign that stated that they served breakfast all day, so that's what I had, breakfast. John had a hot sausage sandwich that would probably feed four men but he finished it. I couldn't get over how fresh the bread was. Even though I was eating breakfast, I think it would have been a sacrilege to toast it. The waitresses moved like lighting—they never wrote anything down when you ordered and cleaning up was not in their job description. I saw one waitress go sailing by, spot a sausage that someone had dropped on the floor and swiftly skootch it under a table with her purple tennis shoes. John told me that all the restaurant help wasn't like this and that they were the exception. He told me that there was a restaurant down here that puts French fries, sour cole slaw, and tomatoes on all the sandwiches they serve, if you want this stuff on it or not. That will be on my next trip. There were shops that sold every kind of nut imaginable. There were also shops that sold nothing but sausage. I can't name all of them but if you're looking for anything in the food line, I would say "The Strip" would be the place to look for it and get it. Depending on the season, there were vendors selling Pittsburgh team apparel at really reasonable prices. That will be another trip—time to investigate a murder.

CHECKING WITH THE CORONER

Time to check with the Peterson's, Doctor Steve, and his gal pal assistant Linda. When John and I entered the lab they were both sweating and I don't think it was that hot in there. I'd hate to think they were doing it in one of the empty coffin carriers. I mentioned this to John and he said that I had a dirty, corrupted mind. Hey, no one is perfect.

I asked the Doc, "Okay, besides being stabbed to death multiple times, how do you think our victim meet her demise?"

The good doctor said, "Miss Reiley was stabbed twenty three times. Usually when there are excessive stab wounds, it indicates that the murderer had an unusual rage toward the victim and took it out on them by the continuing stabbing. But, such was not the case here."

I was intrigued and said, "Why do you say that, Doctor?"

"I'll let my assistant Linda explain it to you," the

good doctor said.

Ms. Peterson said, "Only one stab wound was the cause of death, the one that was thrust into Ms. Reilly's jugular vein. Evidently the killer wasn't too familiar with the human body and added the other stabs to insure the victim was dead. The wound to the jugular was deep while the others tended to be superficial. And by the way, the thrust to the jugular vein was the cause for all the excessive blood on the victims' floor. It appears to me that the killer must have entered through the back door to the kitchen, picked out a murdering tool from the knife rack, entered the dining room and stabbed Ms. Reiley. With that she struggled to flee the house by running toward the front door, while the assailant continued to stab her. That's why the victim's body was found there. We have told you how the victim died, but it is up to you to find out why the victim died. How the victim died is purely conjecture on my part."

I looked at Doctor Peterson and said, "Wow, I didn't know your assistant had a medical and a criminal knowledge background."

The Doc said, "Lin——Ms. Peterson has many medical degrees **and** a degree in criminal technology."

I said, "She should be a helpful asset to the Pittsburgh Police Department." I thanked the doctor and his assistant and John and I took our notes that we had taken and decided to interview a few suspects that we had some interest in. John is going to question Roger Matthew, the high school senior who was constantly giving Rita a hard time. I was going to question John Frey, a well to do married businessman who dated Rita frequently. No one knew why Rita dated John because many times Rita showed up at Joe's for work badly bruised, she had been on a date with

John the previous night. Rita was afraid to confide in her sister, so she always told Gino, believe it or not. I knew this because Gino would call Jean and tell her that John had been batting his sister around. I guess Gino did have a heart—it just wasn't that big. If this jerk, Frey, could beat up on a woman, it's entirely possible he could murder one.

JOHN'S INTERVIEW
WITH ROGER MATTHEWS

John received permission to question Roger Matthew from Carrick High's principal Louis Scott. At first Lou objected to the questioning but after he was informed that John had written permission for the interview from Roger's legal guardian, his grandmother, Sophia Bates, he agreed. Lou arranged to have a room for John's questioning of Roger. John was in the room when Lou brought Roger in. He could tell the kid was trouble when he first looked at him. Principal Scott told him to cooperate with any questions John had.

Roger said, "Why should I? You people can't make me do anything without my grandmother's permission. I've been through this crap before."

John said, "Well smart guy, here is a copy from your grandmother, Sophia, to question you about anything."

Roger said, "That figures. I should have never agreed to move in with that old broad!"

"Well that old broad is the reason you're not in a detention facility for misbehaved little boys like you," I told him.

Both of Roger's parents were incarcerated on drug

offences and the court awarded temporary custody of him until one of them is released. Sophia is Roger's Mother's Mother. {Now there's a little tongue twister for you readers) I guess I could have said grandmother.

John continued, "I understand your grandmother Sophia is the only relative that would agree to be your guardian and you've given her nothing but grief. Anyway, smart guy, I have some questions for you about Rita Reiley and her murder."

Roger said, "Ah, the hot teacher—I've been trying to hook up with her for over a year but she won't have anything to do with me. Why the hell would you be questioning me about her murder—wait, you don't suspect me, do you?"

"Well she surely won't have anything to do with you now, Roger, because she's dead! She was murdered last night in her home."

"And you think I killed her, "Roger shot back. "The next thing you'll be asking me is where I was between so and so hours last night? I assume it was last night. I told you I've been through this crap before."

"Well it's nothing to be proud of that you've been through this (What'd you call it?) crap before," John said. "Actually the approximate time of Rita's death was between 7PM and 11PM last night. Where were you between those times, hot shot?"

"I was on a date—we drank beer, necked, and smoked a little weed on "Lover's Point" in the South Park area of Bethel Park. We were there from I guess 7PM and 11PM last night," Roger smugly replied to John.

John had a big smile on his face and said, "I know that's a bold face lie, loser, because first: I don't think anybody would go out with you on a date and second: who the hell would want to neck with you?"

Roger said loudly, "Hey, what kind of a cop are you, anyway? Aren't you supposed to respect the people that you question?"

John said, "Yea, if those people I'm questioning deserve any respect and you don't seem do deserve any, do you?" Okay, buster, let's have this so called date's name and telephone number so I can verify your so called alibi."

Roger said, "I think her name is Judy, and she's a sophomore at Carrick High. I don't know her phone number or where she lives. I met her at Micky D's last week and we arranged to meet there again last night to go out."

John looked a little pissed and said, "You say that this girl is a sophomore—how old do you think she is and how old are you? If you did go out with this supposed girl and had sexual relations with her, you could be facing a rape charge."

"Relax, Columbo, she had to repeat the ninth and tenth grades a couple of times, so she's plenty old enough for me."

I'm thinking to myself, "Oh great, another mental midget."

John continued, "Were there any other students with you or her, last week or last night when you met her for your big night of kissing, drinking, drugging and whatever else you did?"

Roger said, "Well you know Colonel, I don't recall anyone else being there either of those times. I guess you'll have to take my word for it."

John laughed out loud and said, "Take your word for it. Are you freekin kidding me? Your alibi so far is, you went on a fictitious date, to a fictitious place, with a fictitious girl for four hours. I've been talking to you for fifteen minutes and I can't stand you and you want me to believe you spent four hours with some girl and romanced her. Oh, I'm sorry, you probably don't know what romanced means. I'm going to let you go for now but I'm sure me or my partner will be getting back to you. I know you probably watch a lot of TV, so you'll remember this phrase, "Don't leave town."

MY INTERVIEW WITH JACK FREY (THE MARRIED BUSINESSMAN)

I contacted Jack Frey at his place of employment, Blue Ribbon Insurance—never heard of it, did you? Well they had an office in downtown Pittsburgh. Rent isn't cheap down there, so they must be on the up and up. I put a call into Rita Mancuso, at the station and asked her to check up on this company and also Jack Frey, just in case. I e-mailed John and told him where I was going to be for the next hour. He told me he had wrapped up his questioning with the kid, Roger Matthews. He told me he had a shaky alibi. He also said that he would be at the station for the next hour and was going to enter his notes from the Matthew's questioning. I asked him if he wanted to get some dinner after I was done with John Frey. He said that he had a surprise for me. He had called his parents and they invited us for dinner. I said, "When were you going to tell me?

He said, "I was going to tell you when you got back to the station until you asked me if I wanted to get a bite for dinner. I don't know what my Mother's making, but she's a great cook."

I told John I would see him at the station when I

was done with Frey. I'm thinking to myself, "Ah, a good home made Italian dinner. I haven't had one of those since I left Chicago. I could just taste the tomato sauce."

After I parked in a pay lot I found Blue Ribbon Insurance. It was located in the Oxford building on Grant Street. I called it the Oxford building but it has its name changed a few times since it was called that. The rent in this baby wasn't cheap, I'll tell ya'. Old Frey man must be doing all right for himself. I took the elevator up to the 62nd floor where his office was located. Boy. I just hate heights. I'll try to make this questioning period as short as I can. I introduced myself to John's secretary, Cheryl Hauser. Well that is what was on her desk name plate. Boy, what a set of jugs she had. Hey, that doesn't sound like me or does it? Cheryl was transcribing a letter with a headphone on. Hey, my little two year old niece Lasceona types faster than Cheryl does. She asked me to wait a few minutes until she was done and that she would take me into her bosses' office. At the rate she was typing, my parking tab would be about two-hundred dollars. The city makes us pay for our own parking, damn Mayor Padutti——I bet ya' he doesn't pay for his own parking. Well, back to Ms. Breasts, oops, Ms. Hauser.

My God, Jack Frey was ancient. He had to be at least seventy or seventy five years old. I can see why Cheryl is such a lousy typist. From what I understand, this old fart dated Rita and her step-sister Jean. He must have been doing double duty as a Sugar Daddy. These women must have been desperate, besides being as old as dirt, he was a little on the homely side. Make that a lot on the homely side. Poor guy. Hey, why am I saying poor guy——he's getting more tail than I am. My Mother always hated when I used that word but I got it from my Dad. Oh, I just remembered this is the guy that was supposed to of roughed up Rita a few times. From looking at him, he looks like he'll have trouble picking up his telephone, more less abusing a woman.

I asked Jack if I could call him Jack. He told me that would not be a problem. Then I asked him if he knew why I was there.

"I got a call from a secretary of yours at the Allentown police station, a Rita Mancuso, I think was her name and she filled me in on what I have to expect. I understand that Rita Reiley was brutally murdered last night and you want to question me because I knew her. Am I right so far? Oh, and your secretary sounds hot—do you think I can hook up with her?"

"Yes, she's hot, and very married. Of course that shouldn't bother you—I hear that you have a reputation for romancing younger women, well, younger than you. And I know for a fact that you dated Rita Reiley **and** her sister, Jean."

"You seem to know a lot about me, Lieutenant Patrone."

"I try to be as thorough as I can, Jack, and by the way, that's Sergeant Patrone."But I hope to be promoted to Lieutenant when I nail your ass for Rita's murder. Oh, and by the way, how did you know that Rita was brutally murdered?"

Jack said, "I sell a lot of insurance to members of the police forces and they like to give me little bits of info for a discounted premium, if you know what I mean?"

"Yea, I know what you mean Jack, but I don't think they'll be anymore little tidbits of anything going to your office."

Jack said, "I guess you're looking for my alibi, huh, Sergeant? Well I can tell you that I did date Rita Reiley but I only went out with her sister Jean, once, and that was to a wedding. She had thrown that ass bag husband of hers out for the umpteenth time and she needed an escort for a wedding. Well I can tell you one thing, Sarge, my alibi isn't the best in the world."

"First of all it's Sergeant, not Sarge. And secondly, I've heard nothing but lousy alibis since I started investigating this murder case, so go ahead, give it your best shot! Where were you between the hours of 8PM and 12PM last night?

"Okay, Sergeant, I was at a theater in Bridgeville catching the newest Star Wars flick. I was there from 8:30 PM to 11PM.

"Okay Jack, where you alone or where you with another married woman? And what is the name of the theater, what is the name of the movie, and was the movie any good?"

"I'm sorry, Sergeant, I was alone, I can't remember the name of the theater, or the name of the movie. I do remember that it was very good—much better than the others."

"You call that a decent alibi? You can't remember the name of the theater, the name of the movie and you say you were alone, so you have no one to collaborate your story. The only thing you remember is that it was a good movie—big freekin deal Mr. Frey!"

"Wait a minute, Sergeant, I was at that theater with Rita's sister once—she'll know the name of it."

I said, "Hey lover boy, you said you were only out

with Jean Reiley once and that was when you took her to a wedding. Do you know that first degree murder in this state will get you life without parole? How's that sound, buster?"

"Is there a chance that I can change my story about where I was last night, Sergeant?" Jack said.

"I suggest you better, because the one you gave me sucks and is full of holes."

"Okay, I'm going to be truthful with you Sergeant. I went to Rita's house, had a few drinks and a few budda bings, if you know what I mean?"

"Yea, I know what you mean, go on."

"I left Rita's at 6PM and she was alive when I left. I changed my story about where I was when you told me she had been murdered. I didn't want you to know I was there at all. Is that a little better of an alibi?"

"Not really, hotshot. You don't have anyone to corroborate your statement, because that would be Rita Reiley and she's dead. My partner John or myself will most likely be getting back to you, so keep yourself available and try to keep away from married women or I may be investigating your murder one of these days."

ANOTHER DETOUR, BUT A PLEASANT ONE

I received a text from John telling me that his parents would like to meet me and had invited John and me over to their home in Squirrel Hill for dinner. I was a little confused at first, because I thought the Squirrel Hill area of Pittsburgh was mostly occupied by Jewish families. Boy, I think more like my father every day and I try not to. I really don't care what nationality lives in Squirrel Hill—hey, I was getting a free meal. Then I thought to myself, "Oh great, a homemade Italian dinner. I haven't had one of those since I was home last Christmas." John had told me a few weeks earlier that his parents' names were Gino and Rosa—you can't get much more Italian than that. I know John's mother will be a great cook—I can taste the pasta now.

I met John at the station and we agreed that I would leave my car there and that he should drive. Besides him knowing the area real well, he was driving a Jeep Cherokee with four wheel drive and as always with the Pittsburgh weather, it was snowing and blowing.

John pulled up to his house and pointed out to me that his father had built the house himself from the foundation up. Thank God the long driveway was level leading up to the house. The snow was changing to freezing rain, always a Pittsburgh favorite. It was a beautiful home, in which you can tell it was well taken care of. I pointed this out to John and he thanked me saying that his dad did take wonderful care of his home. As John and I approached the front door and the closer we got to the entrance, I swore I could smell that tantalized smell of Italian food, mostly tomato sauce.

John's father answered the door and immediately gave me a kiss on the cheek and muttered a few Italian words. I'm sorry I never learned any Italian when I lived at home—I was too busy fracturing the English language. I nodded my head at John's father and I could tell by the look on his face, he knew I had no idea what he had said to me. (Switch over to English) John's dad said, "You must be Pete Patrone, my son's partner, and the one who protects his ass every day." Now that I understood, I smiled and said, "Yes,

Mr. Folino, that would be me but I think we sort of try to protect each other's ass.

Mr. Folino rubbed my head with his hand and said, "Let's move to the living room and have a glass of Zinfandel while we wait for our Pizza delivery from Pizza Hut. I just love their Pizza, don't you, Pete?"

"Pizza Hut! Are you shitting me, I'm thinking to myself."

I looked at John's Dad and said, "Yes, Mr. Folino, I love Pizza Hut Pizza," while waiting to be struck dead by the mozzarella gods. Just then John's mom entered the room.

She said to me, "You must be Detective Patrone, the man who's is protecting my son's duppa."

Duppa, now that's one of the words that I do remember as a child. I remember my mother saying to me, "You do that one more time and I'll have your father beat your duppa until it's beet red. I surmised that my duppa wasn't my head, my arms, or my legs, so it must have been my ass. I said, "Yes Mrs. Folino, we try to protect each other. John's a great guy and a great partner."

Mrs. Folino said, "Yes he is. Oh, by the way, did he or my husband tell you the good news?"

What could be worse than "We're having Pizza," I said to myself.

I said, "No, Mrs. Folino, what would that good news be?"

"We're getting Pizza Hut Pizza delivered for dinner. I hope you like it—we all do."

I said, with a straight face, "Oh I do. I eat it all the time!" Thank God they had Zinfandel wine—it sort of eased the pain of eating the Pizza. Don't get me wrong, the Pizza wasn't bad but it wasn't homemade pasta with homemade meat balls and homemade tomato sauce. Oh well, they were nice people and they tried to make me feel at home. After we were done with our Pizza, Mrs. Folino came out with her homemade cannoli's. They were delicious and sort of made up for the Pizza Hut Pizza. I raved about them but told the Folino's I had to get back to the station and pick up my car. I felt bad for John driving in that sloppy crap but he volunteered to drive me to his parent's home. He told me he had to do some paper work and I had some to do as well. Paper work—that never ends when you do police work.

MY INTERVIEW WITH STEPHEN ROSS (RITA'S FORMER LOVER)

John stayed at the station filling out all the necessary paperwork pertaining to the case so far. I was going to call Stephen Ross, Rita's ex-lover and set up a meet. When I called Mr. Ross he begged me not to come to his home. He said he had an extremely jealous wife and if she found out why you were at my home, you might be investigating another murder and believe me, I won't be around for that interview. I appreciated his honesty and was glad I finally was going to question a suspect with a sense of humor, I think. We agreed to meet at a Pancake restaurant, Pamela's in the Mt. Lebanon area outside of Pittsburgh. I'm a breakfast person—I can eat it anytime. I'd rather have a good omelet over a 10 ounce Porterhouse steak. And Pamela's omelets are to die for. Their pancakes are state of the art as well. When I mentioned Pamela's to Mr. Ross, he told me that he was familiar with them and would look forward to our meeting.

I told Mr. Ross that I would meet him at 10:30, a perfect time for breakfast. Mr. Ross said that to recognize him he would be the man with the pink baseball cap. I knew this guy had a sense of humor. He said the cap was a souvenir from his twin boy's tournament for Breast Cancer last year. Wow, a wife and kids—what was he doing messing around with a school teacher?

I walked into Pamela's around 10:20 and there was a man with a pink baseball cap on drinking coffee. I assumed it was Mr. Ross—I mean who else would be goofy enough to wear a pink baseball cap in fifteen degree weather? I walked over to his table and said, "Stephen Ross, I presume?"

He said, "Yes I am. Who else would be goofy enough to wear a pink baseball cap in fifteen degree weather? And by the way, you can call me Steve. And I assume that you are Detective Pete Patrone? You never did tell me how I could identify you but I assume you know that all cops look alike, especially in a neighborhood restaurant and wearing that trench coat you have on."

I smiled a little and said, "You can call me Pete. Let's order first and after we eat we can get to the business at hand."

After we ate, which, by the way was delicious, I asked Steve where he was between the hours of 9PM and 12AM the night of the murder.

He said, "Wow, you don't pull any punches, do you Pete? I can tell you you're going to be disappointed because I have an iron clad alibi—I was in St. Clair's emergency department the night of the murder and my wife drove me there. We were both there from 7PM until 1AM. You see I have problems with kidney stones—sometimes they will pass on their own, but sometime you have to go to the hospital for a little push and pull to get those suckers out. This was one of those nights—I was in extreme pain. See, I told you I you were going to be disappointed in my alibi, didn't I?

I said, "Hell no, I'm not disappointed. In fact yours is the first alibi where someone isn't lying through their eye teeth. I see no point in getting your wife involved in this matter. I'll just check with the hospital to verify your story. You seem like a nice guy—I don't want to investigate your murder. Tell me though, a few things about Rita."

Steve said, "Rita and I had an ongoing affair that ended two years ago when my wife caught us at a restaurant in downtown Pittsburgh. I thought my wife was going to kill her. Thank God she wasn't a client that I was having lunch with. Anyway, my wife gave Rita a hell of a shiner."

I said, "When my partner John and I started investigating this case we saw Rita as a school teacher who worked two jobs to make ends meet, a woman who loved her sister dearly and an all-around nice person. Now as the case goes on, we see a woman who had an affair with a married man and a woman who may or may not been having relations with her sister's husband."

Steve got a little excited and said, "Whoa, don't you believe what that bastard Frank Forbes says about him and Rita. He's full of it. He's been trying to get close to Rita for years but she keeps threatening to tell her sister. That usually ends it for a while or until the next time he gets drunk and horny. And as far as Rita and our affair, we had something grand. Of course I ended it after the confrontation in the restaurant but I decided to end it because of Rob and

Ronnie, our twin boys. Believe me Pete, Rita was a really nice person, except for her alcohol problem and I want you to catch the scum bag that murdered her.

That's the first time I heard anything about Rita's alcohol problem—we'll have to look into that later. I received an e-mail from John telling me to drop whatever I was doing and return to the station. I arrived at the station and went directly to John's office. I asked him what was going on and did he have some startling news for me?

THINGS ARE LOOKING UP— I THINK WE MIGHT HAVE OUR BAD GUY

John said, "I think we've been wasting our time, Pete. We've been treating this murder as though Rita knew her killer. Well the lab reports came in this morning with the DNA results from the crime scene. There were the ones we sort of thought would be there but there was one set of DNA from an ex-con by the name of Jerry Hicks. He had a long list of offences including breaking and entering, assault, robbery and the most important one—"Murder for hire", which we could never pin on him. There just wasn't enough evidence to charge him in that crime. He was charged with B&E and a knife assault in which the victim bled to death. It looks like this could be a random murder or heaven forbid, a murder for hire. We'll know more when we have Mr. Hicks in custody. There's an APB out on him now."

I told John I'd see him in the morning. I planned on going home and seeing if my neighbors wanted to go out and grab a pizza. [You know who I'm talking about—the two hookers.]

I've left the next page blank so you can utilize your dirty minds. And for you righteous church going folks, we went and got a large with everything, chugged a few Iron City's and listened to some oldies. I left them at the pizza joint because I had to get up early. It looks like it may be a promising day. After John and I worked on the never ending paperwork and drank almost a pot of coffee, we got a call from Captain Johnson. He told us that a couple uniforms had picked up Jerry Hicks at a fleabag motel in the North Side of Pittsburgh. The uniforms said that he offered little resistance. I wanted everything by the book on this one, so I had a search warrant drawn up for the suspect's residence. I called Judge Amy Austin and asked her if I could come over to her chambers and have her sign it.

She said, "Of course I'll sign it, but make sure you bring that little cutie, John, with you."

I said, "I'm sure John will like to see Your Honor, again." I knew there was something going on between the two of them a while ago, but I don't know what ended the affair. Oh yea, I know—maybe it was the Judge's husband, Captain Bruce Moonhouser. I told John where we were going to have the warrant signed and he flipped out on me.

"Couldn't you find another judge to sign the papers? You know we had a little thing going on. I really don't want to see that woman and I don't think her husband wants me to see her again either."

I said, "She said she'd signed the papers if you were with me, lover boy. And besides that, she was the only judge available on such short notice."

John said, "Okay, but don't leave me alone with her.

Do you hear me? And quit calling me lover boy."

I said, "Hey, I only called you lover boy one time, lover boy." I could tell he was getting pissed, so I apologized and told him we better get moving.

We arrived at the Judge's chambers about twenty minutes later and she was waiting for us. She looked at me and said, "Hello Detective Patrone, and then looked at John and said, "Hello John."

It was embarrassing watching a grown woman cooing. I wonder what he has that I don't. Oh, I probably can think of a few things but we won't get into that now.

The judge said, "Okay fellas, tell me a little about this case. I already did a search on your suspect—he's a nasty person, isn't he?

We gave her a short history of where we were on the case to this point. She agreed that we should check out the suspect's room before we question him.

As we were leaving her chambers the judge said, "Happy hunting Detectives. Oh, Detective Folino, I'd like to talk to you about something in private. It will only take a few minutes."

I said, "I'm sorry, Your Honor, but we are really in a hurry to search the suspects room, so we can return and begin questioning him."

She said, "Detective Patrone, isn't Detective Folino your superior? I was addressing him, not you."

I'm thinking to myself, "Boy, is this lady a bitch." I then said, "I'm sorry, Your Honor, but Captain Jack Johnson assigned us both to this case as equal detectives in charge. Even though we are equal, I am to learn from Detective Folino's years of experience."

"Well, you should learn to listen to senior detectives," she said. "I said that I want to speak to Detective Folino alone."

Just then a woman on the phone intercom said, "I'm sorry for interrupting you, Your Honor, but your husband is on the line and he says it is important."

The judge says, "Okay Gwen, I'll take it in a minute." She looked at John and said, "I don't want to miss this call, do I detective? I guess I'll get back to the matter I wanted to see you about later. And I hope I don't have to see you again Detective Patrone."

We left in a hurry. [Guess who's on Judge Amy Austin's shit list?]

We arrived at Hicks' apartment about a half hour later. Boy was this place a dump. What was I expecting— the Taj Mahal. We gave a copy of the warrant to the desk clerk. Normally we would have a team of three or four conducting a search but in this case I figured that John and I could handle a one room search. John and I looked in the obvious hiding places and came up empty. We found no knife, drugs or cash. We did find tools frequently used by burglars. We were about to leave when I noticed an envelope corner protruding from under the carpet. I handed it to John who opened it. It was a passbook savings book for a local bank. It showed a deposit of $2,000 a week before the murder. "Where would this jerk face get $2, 000?" I said.

John reminded me that one of the charges against Hicks was *murder for hire*. "I don't think he got this windfall mowing lawns," John said.

The real clincher, and the one that will surely convict Mr. Hicks—there was a Google printout of directions to Rita's house. Now why would this dum-dum hang on to these? We still had time to question Mr. Hicks, so we headed back to the station. I have to admit that we were both looking forward to starting our questioning.

We arrived at the station and told the jailer to retrieve Mr. Hicks and take him to a room we used for interrogations. Hicks was already there, with his legs in shackles attached to the table.

He also was cuffed and there were no windows to aid in an escape attempt. A little bit of overkill on the security but you never know when one of these suspects is going to flip out. We made sure that he was told of his Miranda rights. We also verified that he refused to have Council present at his questioning.

He said, "I don't need an attorney because I'm innocent. I guess you hear that a lot but I am innocent of any charge against me, especially the murder charge. Besides that, I don't have any money and I would need a public defender and we all know that they suck."

John said, "You say you don't have any money. Well we know for a fact that you have $2,000 in the Third Federal Savings and Loan in a passbook savings account."

Hicks seemed surprised and said, "How the hell do you know that? I saved that money from mowing lawns in Mt. Lebanon. (A borough outside the city of Pittsburgh) Besides that, I have my privacy you know."

John and I looked at each other and smiled at the *mowing lawns* comment made by Hicks. It took everything in my power to not bust out laughing. "You lost all privacy when we obtained a search warrant for your apartment," I shot back. "You also lost your privacy when we charged you with breaking and entering and capital murder. When we found the Google directions to the victim's house in that envelope you surely sealed your fate as a convicted murderer. By the way, nice job of hiding that envelope under the carpet, dumb ass."

Hicks looked at both of us and said, "You guys think you know everything, don't you?" I understand that sometimes a deal can be worked out to avoid the death penalty—what do you say?"

Well Mr. Hicks, "That's not up to us—that would be the district attorney, Ruth Rubridge's decision. We would have to contact her and see if she wants to speak with you. You have to have something worthwhile to deal with concerning the charges brought against you. So, tell us, what do you have for us?"

"I can tell you who paid me to kill Rita Reiley", Hicks said.

John and I said, almost in unison, "Who."

Hicks said, "Wait a minute fellas, how stupid do you think I am?"

I wanted to say, "Pretty stupid," but instead said, "Aren't you going to tell us who paid you to kill Rita?"

Hicks said, "When you bring the D.A here, I'll tell you all who paid me to kill what's her name."

I said, "The victim's name was Rita Reiley, you piece of dog doo, and you better have some credible information for us, or I guarantee you, John and I will enjoy watching you die."

"Oh, it's credible all right, and boy are you gonna' be surprised!"

"Cut the dramatics buster", John said. "And pray to God that the D.A. chooses to show you a little more mercy than you showed Ms. Reiley."

We went back to our office and called Ruth Rubridge and asked her if she was familiar with the case. She said she was, and agreed to meet us in the morning. Things were looking up. I asked John if he wanted to stop and get a four dollar cup of coffee at my favorite coffee shop. He declined because he said he had to do some grocery shopping and said it was always a traumatic experience for him. I just said "Okay," and did not elaborate further on his comment.

A DEAL FOR A PIECE OF DIRT

John and I met at the station the next day, and obviously different scenarios went through our minds the night before concerning who might have paid Jerry Hicks to kill Rita Reiley. Boy, were we in for a surprise. And you dear readers, you will be surprised as well.

John and I and the piece of dirt were in the station's small conference room when Ruth Rubridge entered the room. She was a very tall red-haired women with huge blue eyes. Hicks was seated across from me and when he spotted Ruth I thought his tongue was going to fall out and drop on the table. You might call this a minor infraction of police brutality when I kicked him the shins. He let out a yell. I got close to his face and said, "You're not making a good first impression on the woman that holds your life in her hands."

John and I stood up and I grabbed the dirt bag by his collar and pulled him up. I said "Glad to meet you counselor. I understand that you and John are familiar with each other."

Actually, another detective told me that John and Ruth were an item about twenty years ago when he was a rookie and she was working for the public defender's office. From what I understand now, Ruth has been recently divorced. I don't know if John knows this—but if he does I'm sure he may try to rekindle the romance. Getting back to the dirt bag, I said to Ruth, "This is our murder suspect, Jerry Hicks. He's looking to do some dealing today if he has the correct information for us."

Ruth said, "I assumed he is your suspect—after all he is wearing prison garb, isn't he?"

I don't know if she was trying to be funny or just being cute. Nevertheless John and I both let out a little laugh. I said, "Shall we get started?"

Ruth said, "If you gentlemen don't mind, I think I can handle it from here. I've read all of the notes on the case and I know what Mr. Hicks is after."

"Now, Mr. Hicks, exactly what is it that you are after?"

Boy, this woman has a great sense of humor. I can't believe that she and John were an item, because he **doesn't** have a sense of humor.

It was the dirt bags turn to speak. He said, "What kind of deal are you offering me?"

Ruth said, "I understand that you admitted to these two detectives that you savagely murdered Rita Reiley, but that you were paid by another party to commit this crime. Is that correct, Mr. Hicks?"

"Yes it is, Counselor," Hicks replied.

Well normally you would be charged with first degree murder and given the death penalty. But if you agree to reveal who paid you to commit this crime, I will change the charge to second degree murder and recommend to the court that you receive a sentence of twenty to forty years."

Hicks shot back, "What do you mean, recommend?"

Hey, this guy must watch a lot of "Law and Order."

Ruth says, "Believe me Mr. Hicks, if I say the sentence will be twenty to forty years, that's what it will be. A legal document will be drawn up for you to sign. Now that we have that out of the way, who was the person who paid you to savagely kill Rita Reiley?"

Hicks took a huge breath and said, "I don't know why this lady wanted Rita Reiley killed, but she really must have done something pretty bad to piss her off."

Ruth said, "I don't need any sanctimonious crap from you—just give me the name!"

Hicks looked at all of us and said, "It was Rita's step-sister, Jean, you know, the one in the wheelchair. Rita really must have done something to her step-sister to make her resort to murder. I've been meaning to ask you guys, "How did you guys know that I did it?"

John said, "Your prints were all over the place, you yo-yo."

"Yea, I was all spaced out on Crack at the time, otherwise I would have remembered to wear gloves. What an ass I am."

I said, "You got that right, Mr. Hicks. Now, getting back to you and Jean, did her husband, Frank know anything about the murder and tell us in detail how it was arranged?"

Just then Ruth chimed in, "I think you gentlemen are done with me. I haven't included you in that group Mr. Hicks. I have everything I need and I will draw up the papers to have Mr. Hicks sign them. I'm sure I will see you gentlemen again and I know I will see you again, John."

Whoa, it sounds like the romance may be rekindling if John cooperates with the Counselor. We said so long to Ruth and then I repeated my request to Hicks to supply us with details on the night of the crime and details of any meetings with Jean Reiley. I placed a recorder on the table and told Hicks that it would be used as evidence in the crime.

Hicks began with, "I only met Jean Reiley once, and that was to get my payment of Two- thousand. Dollars. She also provided me with Rita's address and when she would be home. I talked to her a few times via e-mail. I got her name and what had to be done from a pal of mine I met at the North Side shelter a few years ago. I paid him a finder's fee of two-hundred dollars for setting me up with the gig. I thought ten percent was reasonable, but he wanted more. I told him ten percent was all I was willing to give him because I had overhead expenses."

I turned off the recorder and interrupted him saying, "What the hell overhead expenses were you talking about? You didn't even buy a knife—you used a butcher knife from Rita's kitchen! After your deposition, I'm going to need the name and address of your shelter friend. Okay, now go on."

He continued, "I'll tell you the guy's name now— his name is Roscoe Ronin. I told him I'd pay him a finder's fee of two hundred dollars to set up the kill of Rita. I figured ten percent was enough. After all, I was doing all the work. I told him if he reported me, he'd be my second victim—he bought that."

Hicks went on, "Jean Reiley called me and told me that Rita called off at Joe's Bar and would probably be home for the night. I drove to her house in this crappy Pittsburgh weather and parked in the back of her house. I drove by the front first to make sure I had the right address. I entered through the back door which was open. Like I said before,

I did a bunch of crack cocaine and wasn't too prepared——I forgot gloves and a knife. I don't own a gun, they scare me.

I'm thinking to myself, "Doesn't this moron ever watch *Murder She Wrote*? The bad guys always wear gloves."

Hicks continued, "When I entered through the rear door I was in the kitchen. I heard what I thought must have been a TV from another room. I spotted one of those chrome racks above a chopper block with a whole bunch of knives on it. I went to crab one and two or three other ones fell on the floor.

Just then Rita came through the adjoining room screaming, "What are you doing in my house?"

I think she must have spotted the big knife in my hand and started to scream. I had to shut her up. The way it went down wasn't my plan. In fact, I really didn't have a plan. Rita then started running down a hallway. I managed to catch up to her and plunged the huge knife into her back. I stabbed her repeatedly. I've never seen so much blood in my life. I think I might have checked her pulse to make sure she was dead and then ran out of the door through the kitchen to my car. There was so much blood!"

I said, "Well Hicks, that's probably all you'll need to get your sweet twenty to forty deal from the D.A. If there's any other questions we'll be sure to be back and see you. Right now Sergeant Folino and I have to go arrest your pal Jean."

John and I didn't figure that Jean Reiley would be going anywhere soon because of her wheelchair. Besides she had no idea we had arrested Jerry Hicks. We thought we'd do a little investigating into Jean Reiley and the circumstances behind why she is confined to a wheelchair.

This normally would have been done earlier but we had no reason to suspect Gene at the time. John agreed to investigate Jean while I worked on the proverbial paper work.

THE MURDERER

From John's digging he found out that Jean was in a near fatal car accident about three years ago. He also discovered that the sweet little school teacher, Rita, had a serious drinking problem. She resided in a local clinic four times in the past five years—she just couldn't give up the hooch. Well this one night a few years ago Rita was attending a party in downtown Pittsburgh. She became hopelessly inebriated and no one would drive her home in the treacherous winter streets of Pittsburgh. No cab service was available either. A guest at the party knew that Rita had a sister and she managed to get her phone number off Rita. When the guest called Jean she was told that the roads were really nasty and she probably could not pick Rita up. After much haggling the guest talked Gene into coming to town to pick Rita up. On the way to downtown, Jean hit an icy spot on the Liberty Bridge and slammed into an abutment. She was rushed to Mercy hospital where she almost died. The ensuing accident, however resulted in the loss of Jean's mobility in both of her legs. She has been confined to a wheelchair since then. Rita was taken to the hospital to see her step-sister by the Pittsburgh Police. They did make a note of their report that Rita was extremely intoxicated when they picked her up at her downtown party. All of this information was available to John in the accident report on file with the Pittsburgh Police Department. The report also revealed that Jean was three months pregnant at the time of the accident and that she lost the fetus at the time of the accident. The report didn't say if Rita was notified of this pregnancy, but I'm sure that Rita was informed by Jean at some time.

John and I had this important info with us when we went to arrest Jean. We had to requisition a large ambulance because of Jean's situation with the wheelchair. One of the EMT's experienced with wheelchair people followed us to Jean's house. John and I talked it over and decided we would also arrest Frank Forbes, Jean's husband as a possible accomplice. Even though Jerry Hicks said that Jean's husband had nothing to do with Rita's murder, we thought we'd question him while we were picking up Jean at her house. Besides that, he could help us to transport Jean to the number one police station. The Allentown station had no facilities to accommodate a wheelchair bound suspect.

Throughout this whole ordeal it never stopped snowing. There must be eight to ten inches out there now. Frank and Jean Forbes lived in the Mt. Oliver section of the city at the top of a steep hill. John was familiar with the street because he had a cousin who lived near there. He said we might have a hard time getting to the top of the street. I had the maintenance man put chains on our squad car. The ambulance was already equipped with chains. When you live in Pittsburgh and you live on one of the many steep hills, you better be equipped for any kind of weather, especially snow, and the number one pain in the butt, freezing rain.

We arrived at the Forbes' home with little trouble, thank God—all that worrying for nothing. Those chains are great but they sure can scratch up your car if you get stuck in the snow somewhere. John knocked on the door of a home that should have been torn down a few years ago. Frank Forbes answered. He said, "Why are you guys here? I paid my fine and spent almost nine hours in the drink tank."

John said, "Actually Frank, we've come here to arrest your wife for contractual murder, but we're arresting you as well as an extra bonus. You see, neither my partner John nor I care much for you."

Just then Jean entered the room in her wheelchair and said, "Did I hear you say you are here to arrest me for murder, whose murder?"

I said, "Come on, Mrs. Forbes, who do you know that has been murdered in the last couple of days—your step-sister, Rita Reiley? We are here to arrest you for contractual murder."

Jean says, "What the hell is that, contractual murder?"

I said, "That means you didn't actually commit the murder, buy you paid someone to do it. Does the name Jerry Hicks mean anything to you?"

"No, it means nothing to me. I thought you were here to arrest my husband for the rape of Rita!"

John and I almost said in unison, "The what?"

"This is the first time either one of us heard anything about any rape. I guess we do have a reason to arrest Frank. I think we'll get into this tomorrow when everybody is fresh."

Frank popped up, "First I get nabbed for a phony drunken arrest and now a rape! What the hell is going on here? And who the hell is Jerry Hicks?"

I said, "Hopefully, we'll get this all cleared up in the morning." The EMT did a fantastic job getting Jean into the ambulance, with a little help from John and I. We put Frank in the back of the squad car in cuffs. We put him in cuffs after we heard of the rape accusation. The EMT dropped off Jean Forbes at the number one station, where Sgt. Phelps received her for incarceration. Then we drove Frank Forbes to our station and tucked him in for the night. I asked John if he wanted to stop somewhere for a drink and he said, "I already have a commitment with Ruth Rubridge."

I said, "You dog, you. When did you get the time to even talk to her?"

John said, "They have this thing called texting, Pete. I've been communicating with her all day."

"Texting, huh, John? I've heard of it but it took me long enough to learn how to send an e-mail.'

John said, "Well you better learn how to text. You'll be using it in the years to come. I'll see you in the morning. Sgt. Phelps is having Jean and Frank Forbes sent up here in the morning so we can start to interrogate them. Who do you want, him or her?"

"I'll take Jean—she sounds pretty feisty", I replied to John. See you in the morning—have a couple of drinks and go right home, by yourself."

Oh God, I sound like his Dad!

I can't believe it stopped snowing. Maybe the city can start cleaning up this crap. I stopped for my usual four dollar cup of coffee. And with that, I received a free refill. Isn't that big of them—it probably cost them twenty cents for the coffee and three to five cents for the water to make it. That's a pretty snazzy profit.

I arrived at the station for a little snow surprise. The city snow removal trucks pushed all the snow in front of our parking lot. I had to park on the street with the commoners. Oh, the humanity!

MY INTERROGATION
OF JEAN FORBES

Our murder suspect was in the larger interrogation room waiting for me. John was in the smaller room with Frank Forbes. We wanted to see what Jean Forbes had to say before we questioned Frank Forbes.

I said good morning to Jean Forbes and asked her if she wanted a cup of coffee. She thanked me and said that she already had two cups at the number one station. I placed a tape recorder on the table and informed her that everything from now on would be recorded and could be used against her at a later time. I asked her if she had any problems with the accommodations at the number one station.

She said "I assume you don't have too many handicapped people incarcerated in your jail downtown, do you? And the food absolutely sucked. I mean, I haven't had a fried baloney sandwich in years. And to top it off, they slopped mustard on it, not ketchup or mayo, mustard!"

If she thinks that was bad, wait until she's convicted of murder and sent to Muncie Woman's prison—she'll be lucky if they even have mustard. In response to her initial question I said, "No we don't have too many handicapped people incarcerated at our number one station. Most of the handicapped people that are charged and sent downtown are drug related offences, and after they are processed and charged they are usually sent to a hospital under guard until they are arraigned for their crime. But your case is a little unusual—a capital murder, and besides that, you had to be transferred here for questioning. I think I'll begin my questioning now, Jean."

"You do know that we have Jerry Hicks under arrest, and that he has indicated that it was you who paid him $2,000 to brutally murder your step-sister, don't you? Oh, and I do mean brutally—I can show you some police photos if you wish?"

"No, I don't wish to see any photos," Jean said. "And as far as this business with Jerry Hicks, I can deny I knew him but I know how you cops operate. You probably gave him a lie detector test and offered him a sweet deal of some kind. Well, what's your name again?"

"Detective Sergeant Pete Patrone, Ma'am."

Jean went on, "Well Detective Pete Patrone, I want a sweet deal too."

I said, "Sorry Jean, the dealing is done—you have nothing to deal with. We have Mr. Hicks' confession implicating you in Rita's murder. And my partner is next door questioning your husband about the murder."

"Well you're not going to get anything out of him about the murder, because he didn't know anything about my plans with Hicks. But I want to see him go to the prison for raping Rita and contributing to the reason I decided to have my step-sister killed, among other things."

"What do you mean, *among other things*?"

"Well you do know that Rita was pregnant with my husband's child, don't you?" Rita said. The sleaze ball raped Rita a few months ago but it wasn't until last week that Rita called and told me that she was pregnant. I don't know what kind of records you keep here, but I'm assuming that you know I was on my way to pick up my drunken step-sister when I crashed on the Liberty Bridge. Well you should also know that I was pregnant and lost my child. Boy, that husband of mine is a fertile bastard, isn't he?"

Jean went on, "When Rita told me she was pregnant and Frank was the father, I really didn't care that Frank was the father. Mickey Mouse could have been the father for all I cared. The fact that she was going to have a child is what really bothered me. You see, I **had** to kill her. She ruined my life and my future child's life. Now that she was going to have a child just didn't sit right with me. And the fact that I have to spend the rest of my life in a wheel chair is also a very tough pill to swallow, while she is out guzzling all the booze she can get her hands on. I know for a fact she never quit drinking."

I looked at her in disgust and said, "When I first started investigating this case, it was all about the love you two sisters had for each other. What happened?"

"Hate can change a lot of things Detective."

I said, "You know, Miss Forbes——"

"Call me Jean."

"You know, Jean——there may be a way for you to get a reduced sentence. You are definitely going to spend time in prison no matter what. I can talk to the D.A. and see if you wave a jury trial and plead guilty, you can receive a reduced sentence. I see that you refused the use of a public defender but if I get you any kind of deal, you may need one——it's up to you. We'll see what your husband has to say and then we'll get back to you."

JOHN AND MY QUESTIONING OF FRANK FORBES

I met John out in the hall of the station and told him we had to talk. I told him the reason why Jean Forbes killed her step-sister. She blamed Rita for her spending the rest of her life in a wheelchair. He also said that Rita called her about a week before the murder and told her that Frank had raped her and that she was pregnant with his child. She also indicated that the fact that Jean was pregnant was another reason she paid Hicks to kill her. "These are some evil back-stabbing women we're dealing with here," John. I suggested we go in and see what Frank Forbes has to stir the pot a little more.

No intros were needed because Frank Forbes had met both of us already. I started the questioning of Frank. I said, "Okay, Frank, tell us about the rape."

He said, "What rape?"

I said, "Come on Frank, your wife said that Rita called her and told her she was pregnant with your child because you had raped her."

Frank said, "Believe me pal, all the sex I had with Rita was—what's that word?"

"The word is consensual, Frank, and remember one thing, I am definitely not your pal! Okay, you can continue."

Frank went on, "Like I was saying, all the sex I had with Rita was consensual. She would be home slopping up the hooch and feeling sorry for herself and then call me up for a quickie. It had to be a quickie because when she called me on my cell, I'd make up an excuse and tell my wife I had to go out for something and would be right back. This happened a couple times a week. No wonder she got pregnant. I'll tell you though, I really felt bad lying to my wife like that."

I said, "Give me a break. Frank. I can't see you feeling sorry or feeling bad for anyone. The sad part here is, we have no way to prove you raped Rita. A paternity test on the fetus will confirm that it was your child, but again, we can't prove if the sex you had with Rita was consensual or not. I believe you are a piece of dirt, Frank, and that the sex you had with Rita was consensual. And I also believe that Rita's death can be equally shared with your wife, for whatever twisted justice she imagined she did in having Rita murdered."

I looked at John and asked him if he had anything else for Frank.

He said "I agree with you, Pete—we are facing a little glitch with this rape thing. There is no way to prove that Rita was raped. I looked back at my notes and saw where Frank told us, 'On the night of the murder that he stopped at Rita's from time to time for a little companionship. I think we're going to probably have to release this piece of shit because we have nothing to charge him with. His wife already said that he knew nothing about her dealings with Jerry Hicks."

I said, "John, I think you're right, I'll see the desk sergeant and have his release papers drawn up. How about calling your girlfriend at the DA's office and see if we can offer Jean Reiley some kind of deal for pleading guilty."

SNAFU

It appears that Jean Reiley did not want a deal that the state was offering: twenty years to life. At least she would not have faced the death penalty if she takes a deal. Jean exercised her constitutional right to have a court appointed attorney. I'm assuming she is counting on the sympathy of the jury. After all she is confined to a wheelchair and has a pig for a husband. We'll see what we shall see.

JEAN REILEY AND HER ATTORNEY

In our judicial system, when the accused asked for a public defender they are assigned one from a pool of attorneys available for defending capital cases. Jean drew a good one, Harvey Goldstein. Harry had the reputation of being a good attorney with a winning track record. On Harry's initial visit with Jean he told her he would emphasize her disability, and the fact that she was married to a no-good cheating slob who had relations with his wife's half sister. (Sounds familiar, doesn't it?)

Harry sat down with Jean and said, "You do realize that by turning down the deal with the DA, there is a possibility that you could receive the death penalty if you are found guilty of first degree murder. But I wouldn't count on it—none of my past clients have ever received a death sentence, whether if they were guilty or innocent."

Jean said, "Well that's very reassuring, Mr. Goldstein."

Harry said, "Well Jean, I see where your partner in crime did the smart thing and took the DA's deal. I've looked at his confession—to be rather blunt, he really put the screws to you, Jean. I know you've read the transcript of the Mr. Hicks confession—now tell me, is there anything that Hicks was lying about or may have missed in his confession?"

Jean said, "I'm afraid everything he said was true."

Harry said, "Well that's about it, Jean. I just hope we have a sympathetic jury."

It turns out they *did* have a sympathetic jury. They found Jean guilty, but without the extenuating circumstances. Would you believe they chose to be lenient—Jean received a ten to twenty year sentence without the life term stimulant? This was half of what the DA had proposed. Harry Goldstein was very happy, Jean was very happy, and the DA Ruth Rubridge was very mad.

WRAPPING IT UP

I asked John what he thought of the verdict and sentence.

He said, "That most cases, especially murder cases, don't wind down this quickly. He said that if it wasn't for deals from the DA, cooperation from prosecution and defense attorneys, we would spend seventy-five percent of our days in courtrooms. We know the deal that Jerry Hicks received, twenty to forty years. We couldn't charge Jean's husband, Frank, with anything, although this whole mess started with his rape/no-rape of Rita's step-sister, Jean. Now for the main character, Jean Forbes, who should have been charged with first degree murder—first degree murder with extenuating circumstances, thirty years, with no chance for parole. These lawyers crack me up—in order to avoid the death penalty for Jean, the DA threw in *extenuating circumstances*. Somehow they intertwined these circumstances into the original charges and came up with the thirty year term. From what I understand, Jean Forbes was a hell of a knitter—well she'll have at least thirty years to improve her craft. I understand that they have expert accommodations for handicapped offenders. Jerry Hicks will get lost in the Pennsylvania prison system, and Frank Forbes will enjoy his gift of undeserved freedom.

A couple of weeks after all the legal mumbo jumbo was worked out, I received a request from the Chicago

Police Department. They had read about my work on the Rita Reiley murder case and requested if the Allentown Police Department could release me temporarily to work on a murder that was committed at a beauty pageant. Captain Elam told me he'd be sorry to lose me, but he thought it would be a good experience for me. I told John of my plans and he said that he was very happy for me. I thanked him for all the help he gave me in the Reiley case and wished him well with the DA. He knew what I was talking about.

Epilogue (Two years later)

We'll start with a couple minor characters in our little story, Dr. Steve Peterson, Allegheny County Coroner, and Linda Peterson. They decided to abandon their respective mates and cut and dissect corpses as husband and wife.

Gino Riggerio, the owner of Joe's bar, and Rita Reiley's part time employer. Six months after Jean Forbes entered prison he was robbed at his tavern and shot and mortally wounded.

Johnny Stanko and Eddie Edosia, the two bar patrons at Joe's Bar, purchased Joe's after Gino was mortally wounded in a robbery. They remodeled the tavern, expanded the menu and opened two more locations. They still serve the best hot sausage in the South Hills.

Bill Evans and Omar Pack, the two neighbors of Rita's, formed a bowling team called "You'll Get Yours," and dominated the bowling scene at Noble Manor Lanes in Crafton, Pa. for years to come.

Roger Matthews, the senior who had the hots for Rita, attempted to rob a beer distributor two doors from the Allentown Police Station, and was shot in the process. He survived, and is serving two to five years in Green County State Correctional Institute. (I think he'll do the five)

Louis Scott, Carrick High School Principal, was appointed Pa. Education Director.

Jack Frey, the married businessman, who dated Rita, among other woman, was caught by his wife, Mona, in a very compromising position, and shot eight times, two in a very crucial spot. He did not survive.

Stephen Ross, Rita's ex-lover, was fatally stabbed by his wife after she read some incriminating sexual messages on his e-mail account.

Judge Amy Austin, the judge who issued the warrant for Jerry Hicks, ran successfully for deputy governor of Pennsylvania, under the Democratic platform.

Capt. Jack Elam, Allentown police chief, was transferred to the downtown number one station, where he is to this day. He took Rita Mancuso, Allentown's secretary, with him, after she divorced her husband, Jim.

Allegheny County District Attorney Ruth Rubridge, moved to a small home down the street from her in-laws, Gino and Rosa Folino, in the Squirrel Hill area outside of Pittsburgh. Yes, after an almost two year courtship, John Folino married the DA, Ruth Rubridge.

Attorney Harry Goldstien, successfully defended Mona Frey, on the murder of her husband, Jack. (The charge—justifiable homicide)

The End

Other Titles by Ed Folino

Long Time Coming, Volume 1

Long Time Coming, Volume 2

Murder at the Library, x2

My Pittsburgh

Murder on a Cruise and The Murdered Queen

Words From My Mind

www.ingramcontent.com/pod-product-compliance
Lightning Source LLC
Chambersburg PA
CBHW051927220626
47052CB00003B/604